Oh No! Where did Walter Go?

Joanna Boyle

 templar publishing

This is Olive

and this is Walter.

They are **best** friends and partners in crime.

They are also . . .

acrobats

detectives

explorers

and pirates!

Olive is the Master of Mystery
and Walter is the Duke of Daring.

Oh no!
Where did
Walter
go?

. . . but Walter was nowhere to be found!

Outside, the city was busy and loud and large.
Olive couldn't see Walter anywhere.
"I'll have to find him!" she cried,
and she dashed out the door.

Olive searched
the city like a
good detective.

She followed suspicious footprints,

collected evidence

and talked to locals.

She even stuck posters on every wall, but Walter could not be found at all.

It really didn't help that there were
so many cars zooming about . . .

. . . and so much screeching and beeping.

And there were SO MANY people pushing and shoving and shouting.
Fortunately Olive had a BIG pirate voice.

But it was all getting just a bit . . .

Luckily, help was at hand!

I saw a parakeet heading towards the park!

Olive knew it would take ages
to find the park in these
criss-crossing streets . . .

. . . so she climbed up
something tall (just like
an acrobat would).

When Olive reached the park she peered inside.
The trees were towering and it looked like a very easy place to get lost.

Inside, the park was gigantic and green.
How would Olive find a tiny green
parakeet in all this?

Olive looked for Walter everywhere.

She explored dark and scary places.

She climbed up trees and peered under hedges.

But would the Master of Mystery
give up on the Duke of Daring now?
No . . . she would not.

But explorers go to new places even when they're scared,
so Olive pushed open the gate.

She followed trails and questioned witnesses.

She took note of anything suspicious.

But he was nowhere to be found. And soon Olive realised . . .

. . . that she was completely lost.
Olive's lip trembled.

Olive's shouting had startled the birds in the trees.
There were HUNDREDS OF PARAKEETS!
Olive would never find Walter now!

But wait! Who was that flying in a different direction from the rest?

It was WALTER!
"I've been looking for you everywhere!" cried Olive.
"I've been looking for *you* everywhere!" cried Walter right back.

The Master of Mystery and the Duke of Daring made their way home.
It wasn't easy and they got lost quite a few more times . . .

BARK BARK!

But for some reason neither of them
seemed to mind too much.

And finally . . .

. . . they made it home
safe and sound.

While Olive was looking for Walter, Walter was looking for Olive too! Did you see him on every page?

A TEMPLAR BOOK

First published in the UK in 2017 by Templar Publishing,
an imprint of Kings Road Publishing,
part of the Bonnier Publishing Group,
The Plaza, 535 King's Road, London, SW10 0SZ
www.bonnierpublishing.com

1 3 5 7 9 10 8 6 4 2

ISBN 978-1-78370-631-0

Edited by Katie Haworth
Designed by Olivia Cook

Printed in China

For my
fantastic
granny,
love Jo xxx

More picture books from Templar:

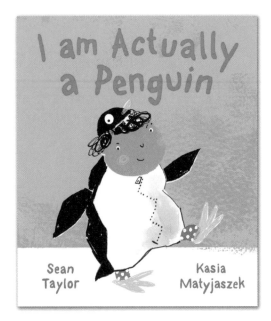

ISBN: 978-1-78370-451-4 (paperback)

ISBN: 978-1-78370-801-7 (paperback)

ISBN: 978-1-78370-800-0 (hardback)

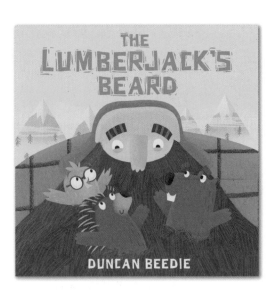

ISBN: 978-1-78370-687-7 (hardback)
978-1-78370-688-4 (paperback)